W9-AQG-581

The Silver Balloon

THE SILVER BALLOON

Story and Pictures by Susan Bonners

Farrar Straus Giroux • *New York*

Special thanks to Patricia J. Wynne
and Ivy Rutzky

Library of Congress Cataloging-in-Publication Data
Bonners, Susan.
    The silver balloon: story and pictures / by Susan Bonners. — 1st ed.
        p.   cm.
    Summary: When fourth-grader Gregory releases a helium-filled
balloon into the sky with his name and address attached, it leads to
an unusual friendship and an exchange of mystery gifts.
    ISBN 0-374-36913-5
    [1. Natural history—Fiction.   2. Friendship—Fiction.
3. Libraries—Fiction.]   I. Title.
PZ7.B64253Si   1997
[Fic]—dc20   96-30895

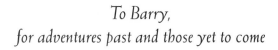

To Barry,
for adventures past and those yet to come

Contents

The Silver Balloon

Sail Away

One evening in early September, Gregory sat by his bedroom window, watching the sky darken. A pigeon wheeled overhead. Gregory imagined himself flying over the tall buildings, out beyond the last city rooftops, flying to an unexplored land of forests and mountains where animals prowled the night.

Absentmindedly, he played with the dangling string of the silver helium balloon he'd gotten at the shoe-store opening that afternoon. The balloon was bobbing gently against the ceiling, like an animal looking for a way out of its cage.

How far up could it go if someone let it out the window? Would it ever come down? Could it sail away to some other country?

Gregory dumped the contents of his desk drawer onto his bed. He found an index card and printed his name and address on it. Then he punched a small hole through the card and threaded the balloon string through it, tying a secure knot.

His admission tag from the natural history museum lay on the heap. He taped it to the card. Whoever found it would know something about him.

He raised the screen. Now he was sending his balloon off on a great adventure.

The balloon drifted up as if pulled by an invisible string, up and up until it was a tiny dot of silver among the twinkling stars. Then it disappeared.

"Any answer yet?" asked Tommy on the way home from school one Friday.

Gregory shook his head without looking up. Three weeks had gone by. His beautiful balloon must be flattened on a rooftop somewhere or snagged on a TV aerial.

They walked the rest of the way to Gregory's building in silence. That was one of the things Gregory liked about his friend. Tommy didn't mind when a person was quiet.

Gregory reached for his front door key and said, "Mrs. Nelson's probably sleeping on the sofa." Mrs. Nelson stayed with Gregory every day until his mother got home from her job at the Red Rose Restaurant.

They tromped up the stairs to the fourth floor. Mrs. Nelson was leaning out of the doorway to Gregory's apartment, smiling and waving an envelope.

"It's for you! As I recall, someone in this family was awfully anxious to get a letter."

Gregory ran down the hall. "Thanks, Mrs. Nelson." Carefully, he opened the envelope so he wouldn't tear the return address.

"It's the card I sent with the balloon!"

He turned it over. A name was printed on the back.

Clarence ("Pete") Mayfield

Taped under the name was something that looked like the top of a weed.

Mrs. Nelson pointed to the return address. "This is over the state line, but I have no idea where. I've never heard of Porter's Mills."

"And what's that thing he sent?" asked Tommy.

"Mrs. Nelson," Gregory said, stuffing the card into his knapsack, "we have to go to the library. We'll be back later."

At the library, Mrs. Twombly set the atlas in front of them with a thud. They rolled back the slick pages until they got to the map of the right state.

Gregory and Tommy had spent lots of after-noons at this same table, reading books and maga-zines about adventures in the wilderness and plan-ning the camping trips they would take when they were older.

They began to search the map, back and forth, then up and down. They worked in circles. They worked in squares. The minutes ticked by. Then Gregory got the idea to follow the rivers. He slid his finger along a dozen squiggly black lines before he saw it.

"Tommy, here it is." On a winding river, "Porter's Mills" was printed in tiny letters.

"It must be really small," said Tommy. "I bet there's about three houses in the whole town."

No large cities were marked nearby. "Do you suppose that's all woods?" Gregory said, pointing to the empty space above the river.

"I don't know. Why would he send a weed?"

"It's some kind of clue."

"Let's figure it out at my house, Greg. We can get something to eat."

Gregory lugged the atlas back to the front desk. "Thanks, Mrs. Twombly."

"You're welcome, Gregory."

As they walked out the door, Tommy asked, "Did you figure out the barrel hitch yet?"

Gregory set down his knapsack and pulled out a worn copy of *Knots Every Outdoorsman Should Know.* "No, but I've almost got it." He found the page.

"What about the bowline? We'll need that if we have to haul our gear up a cliff."

"That one's easy. I'll show you later."

At Tommy's, Gregory put his knot book and

index card on the kitchen table. As Tommy got o
the peanut butter and bread, his grandmother can
into the kitchen and sat down.

"*Buon giorno! Come stai,* Gregory?"

"I'm fine, Mrs. Santoro. How are you?"

"Oh, good, good."

Mrs. Santoro lived with Tommy and his mother
Tommy didn't have a father. That was another rea
son why he and Gregory were best friends. Ever
though Tommy's father just lived someplace else—
he hadn't died like Gregory's had—that made them
a lot alike.

"*Buon giorno,* Nonna," said Tommy. He handed
his grandmother the card. "Gregory got this in the
mail. Because he sent the balloon. The *palloncino,*
Nonna. I told you about it."

She nodded. "Oh, *si.*" Fingering the weed, she
said, "*Grano.*"

"What, Nonna?" said Tommy. "I don't think I
know that word."

"*Grano,*" she said again. "You know . . ."

"Is that some kind of weed, Mrs. Santoro?"

"No, is not."

9

"A tree?" Tommy suggested. She shook her head.

"A flower?" Gregory asked.

Mrs. Santoro looked around the kitchen impatiently. Suddenly she grasped the loaf of bread. *"Grano,"* she said, holding it up.

"I'm sorry, Mrs. Santoro. I don't understand."

"Wait a minute, Greg. I just remembered. She's saying 'wheat.' That's what the bread's made out of. We've solved part of the mystery!"

"Grazie, Mrs. Santoro. Thanks a million!"

An Unsolved Mystery

That evening, while his mother washed the supper dishes, Gregory sat at the kitchen table, fiddling with his pencil and staring at the yellow lined paper in front of him. The printing on the card looked like a grownup's. He'd never written to a grownup he didn't know. He almost never wrote to anybody, except for notes to Tommy in their secret code, but that didn't count.

"Just write the way you'd talk to someone," his mother said.

That didn't help much. When Gregory had to

talk to people he didn't know very well, he got nervous and tongue-tied.

"Pretend you're talking to Tommy."

He began.

Dear Mr. Mayfield,

Thank you for the wheat. Are you a farmer? My friend Tommy and I found your town on a map. It looked really small. Do you live near the woods?

"Why don't you tell Mr. Mayfield about your rock collection? And your plants? And your ants? That's so interesting."

Mr. Mayfield probably wouldn't care about those things, but Gregory had to write something.

I'm studying about plants and animals on my own. I grew a grapefruit plant from a seed and I have an ant farm. I'm saving up for a fish tank.

Yours truly,
Gregory Kepler

He wanted to send a small gift, too, something

for Mr. Mayfield to figure out. He thought about it the rest of the evening.

The next morning, as he scooped up his pocket change, he noticed a bus token. Mr. Mayfield lived so far away he probably never came to the city. Gregory slipped the token into the envelope and added a line to the letter.

P.S. Here is a Mystery Gift for you.

After school on Tuesday, Gregory heard running feet behind him.

"Slow down, Greg. There can't be any answer yet. You just mailed that thing on Saturday."

But Gregory flipped through the stack of mail on the hall table anyway.

"I'm afraid not, Gregory."

Mrs. Nelson was "afraid not" on Wednesday, Thursday, and Friday, too.

On Saturday morning, Gregory sat lost in thought. Shirts, socks, towels, and pillowcases swirled around in the triple-loader in front of him. As he stared at the tumbling forms, he thought of his balloon tumbling in the wind, then falling, falling, falling into a golden field of wheat. At the edge of the field, a whitetail buck plunged out of the forest, then stood motionless. Above him, a great horned owl roosted on the bough of a balsam fir, waiting for night.

"I think the rinse cycle is over, Gregory," said his mother. "Bring me that cart, will you?"

Gregory sighed and slid off his chair. He yanked the battered plastic cart across the floor. The wheels kept twisting the wrong way. He kicked at them. Mr. Mayfield probably wouldn't write back.

But the letter was waiting when Gregory and his mother got home from the laundromat.

Dear Gregory,

Thanks for the bus token. At first, I thought it was an old coin, but Mrs. Connors at the P.O. knew what it was. It will come in handy if I ever get to the city!

Glad to hear you're interested in nature. I learned

*quite a bit on my own, too, when I was younger. Then
I took over on the farm after my father hurt his back and
I've been farming ever since.*

*Yes, there's some woods around here. Not as much as
there used to be. There's a nice stretch near the river where
I used to camp.*

Yours,

Pete Mayfield

*P.S. I'm sending along a Mystery Gift, too. Maybe you
know what these are.*

Four little red balls rolled out of the envelope.

"Mom, are these cherry tomatoes? They're kind
of small."

"No. They're sort of like cranberries, but they're
not. They're not like any kind of berry I know
about."

Gregory ran to Tommy's with the letter.

"See? He used to camp, just like we're going to
do."

When Tommy showed the red balls to his
grandmother, she shrugged and shook her head.

At the library, Gregory emptied the envelope

into Mrs. Twombly's hand. "Let's see. Berries grow on bushes. We have a book on shrub identification with the field guides."

They brought the book to their table.

"Greg," said Tommy, after a few minutes, "these things all look alike to me. Can't you just ask him?"

"No." Gregory couldn't explain, but he had to get this on his own. Otherwise, Mr. Mayfield would think he didn't know anything about studying nature. He wouldn't want to continue the game.

"I've got it. Ask Mr. Hansen. A teacher ought to know about stuff like this."

That was an idea. But Gregory still wanted to figure out the gift by himself. Besides, school had just started a month ago. He didn't know Mr. Hansen, his fourth-grade teacher, very well yet.

"I'll ask him if you want," Tommy said when Gregory didn't answer.

"No, that's okay."

"It's Saturday, Greg. There's probably a game in the park. We can figure this out later."

"You go. I'll be there in a couple of minutes."

Tommy stood up. "You're really coming, right?"

Gregory nodded.

Alone, he flipped through a few more pages. Tommy was right. All the pictures started to look alike.

Maybe he'd see something at a store that would help. He left the library and walked down Center Street. He stood in front of the fruit stand.

"Can I help you?" asked the man.

"Uh, no, thanks," Gregory mumbled. He kept going.

He went up the produce aisle at the grocery store. He looked in the window of the fancy-food store. At last, he headed for the park.

Maybe he'd have to ask Mr. Hansen.

Searching

On Sunday morning, Tommy's grandmother came to the door of their house in answer to Gregory's special tap on the window.

"*È malato,*" she said, touching her throat and ear.

Gregory understood that Tommy had one of his earaches with a sore throat. When he wasn't in school on Monday, Gregory knew he'd be in bed for a long time.

When the last bell rang on Monday afternoon, Gregory took a few minutes arranging his books. Everybody in his row pushed past him.

"Stampede!"

"Jailbreak!"

The last child skipped out the door. Mr. Hansen was clipping papers together. Gregory would ask him now.

Sheila McIntyre ran back into the room.

"Mr. Hansen, I don't understand about the lowest common denominator. Would you explain it again?"

"Of course. Just a minute, Sheila. Gregory, did you want to talk to me?"

"Me? No." Gregory hoisted his knapsack onto his shoulder and walked out. Why was it easy for other people to ask for help?

He pounded down the stairs and headed up the avenue toward his street. At the next corner, instead of staying on the avenue, he turned right onto a quiet block, not sure what he was looking for. Something. He turned down the next side street and the next.

The houses here were all connected, their tiny front yards covered with cement. Here and there, window boxes decorated the somber housefronts.

Otherwise, nothing grew. Even the weeds in the sidewalk cracks had been pulled out.

Gregory stopped at the last house on Hanover Place. This yard was different, crowded with planters in the shape of animals. Ducks, a donkey, swans, geese, and an elephant all jostled for space. A rosebush growing out of the elephant bobbed in the wind. Soon, the last of the withered blossoms would drop. Where they had fallen off, the stems ended in little red balls—just like the ones Gregory had in his pocket.

He glanced up at the windows. The blinds were closed. Whoever lived there probably wouldn't mind if he took one of the balls, the one poking through the iron fence. He gave a gentle tug and it popped off.

Gregory ran all the way to the library.

"On a rosebush?" said Mrs. Twombly. "Come." She walked to the shelf labeled GARDENING and pulled out a fat volume. "Roses . . . roses . . . Here." She pointed to a photograph.

Gregory read the caption: "The seeds of the rose are contained in fleshy fruits called rose hips. Rose

hips are sometimes used as an ingredient in herb tea."

Using Mrs. Twombly's letter opener, they cut open the rose hip that Gregory had found and one of Mr. Mayfield's Mystery Gifts. The insides were identical.

"Thanks, Mrs. Twombly!"

Gregory wrote a coded message for Tommy and dropped it in his mailbox on the way home. He could hardly wait to write to Mr. Mayfield. But what gift could he send this time?

In the days that followed, wherever Gregory went, his eyes were open for the right object. He began to see things he'd never noticed before.

"Did you know there's a dragon on top of the bank?" he asked his mother at supper Tuesday evening.

"Is this some kind of riddle?"

"No, there's really a dragon. It's got wings and claws and everything."

"Oh, you mean like a gargoyle or something? Well, I'll have to look next time."

On Wednesday, Gregory watched workers from

the electric company unroll wire from a giant spool on the back of a truck. On Thursday, he saw a door knocker in the shape of a lion's head.

But he couldn't send these things, and he didn't have a camera. By now, Mr. Mayfield must be wondering where the letter was.

A cold drizzle was falling as Gregory walked home on Friday. He dumped his books on his desk and flopped on the bed.

Mrs. Nelson appeared in the doorway. "Can I get you a snack?"

"No, thanks, Mrs. Nelson. I'm not hungry."

After a few minutes, Gregory got up and took down a shiny cardboard box from his closet shelf. He gently pried off the lid. On a bed of crumpled tissue paper was the prize of his nature collection, the nest of a paper wasp.

One April morning, he'd noticed a wasp making trip after trip to a spot under a first-floor windowsill on his building. Then he saw she was making a nest there. From his insect book, Gregory knew that she was forming it out of delicate layers of paper that she made by chewing wood. He'd watched her raise a colony of wasps that summer. By late fall, they had all disappeared. Then he and Tommy had reached the nest by hauling two big crates from the alley to climb on.

He could send the nest to Mr. Mayfield, but he didn't know when he'd be able to get another, maybe never. It was the best thing he had ever found. He put the lid back on the box and put it in the closet again.

He decided to talk it over with Tommy. He hoped Tommy was feeling better. School hadn't been much fun without him.

On Saturday morning, as he waited at his corner for the light to change, Gregory found himself staring at a manhole cover. He'd never noticed before that some of the raised letters on it read PRODUCT OF INDIA. A manhole cover had come halfway around the world. Mr. Mayfield would probably think it was interesting, too, but Gregory couldn't send it to him.

Suddenly Gregory remembered something he had read. He ran back upstairs, grabbed a pencil and sharpener out of his desk, taped together four sheets of paper, and ran down to the street.

Luckily, the manhole cover was next to the curb, so he didn't have to worry about cars. But holding down the paper in the wind was going to be a problem.

"What're you doing, Greg? Need some help?"

Tommy stood over him, wearing a pair of blue earmuffs.

"They look really stupid, don't they? My mother made me put them on."

"Can you just hold these two corners down?"

Tommy was good at helping with things. He didn't keep asking why you had to do a thing a certain way.

Gregory began stroking the paper with the side of his pencil. Where the pencil hit the letters and designs, it made a mark. Together, the marks made a picture. Gregory had to keep sharpening his pencil until it was almost gone, but every last letter came out.

"I read this is the way to copy the writing off an

old gravestone. It's Mr. Mayfield's next Mystery Gift."

"Great idea. I wonder if he'll ever figure it out."

That night, Gregory wrote his second letter. This one was easier than the first. He even enjoyed writing it.

Dear Mr. Mayfield,

Thanks for the rose hips. I found some more of them growing on a rosebush right here in my neighborhood. Then I read about them in a book.

I forgot to tell you before, I have a rock collection, an animal picture collection that I cut out of magazines, and a piece of coral that I got for a present.

Do you think you'll ever go camping again?

Your friend,

Greg

P.S. I'm sending your next Mystery Gift.

Hand Cancel

Mr. Mayfield's second letter took longer to arrive than the first. It was waiting for Gregory after school on a Thursday afternoon.

Dear Greg,

You really gave me a puzzle this time. I might never have figured it out, but Mr. Campbell, the garage mechanic, used to work for the power company and he knew that it was a manhole cover. Clever! Why do you suppose they make those things in India?

Sometimes I think about going camping, but some-

thing always seems to get in the way. After I got your letter, I found my old camp stove in the shed and my fry pan and my coffee pot. Those days sure were fun.

Yours,

Pete

P.S. I found your next Mystery Gift on a fishing trip up north. Be careful when you handle it so you don't cut yourself. It's something special. I think you're someone who will know the value of it.

The envelope had been marked "Hand Cancel." Inside was a small, flat box. When Gregory lifted the lid, he found a brownish-gray leaf-shaped object that was hard and a little shiny, with sharp ridges all over it. Mr. Mayfield had cushioned it with a cotton ball.

"I don't suppose you're going to find one of these growing in somebody's yard," Tommy said when Gregory put it in his hand later that afternoon.

At the library, Mrs. Twombly had a long line of people at her desk. Gregory and Tommy sat down at their usual table. Tommy looked in the box.

"Is it some kind of rock?"

"He said it was special. Maybe valuable."

"Like silver or gold? It doesn't look like silver or gold," Tommy said.

"Wait a minute. When they find that stuff in mines, isn't it sort of dirty-looking? Let's go find a picture."

On the shelf labeled EARTH SCIENCES, they found photographs of gold ore and silver ore—lumpy, twisted masses of metal.

"A piece of stalagmite?" Tommy suggested.

They looked farther along the shelf. Gregory found a book on caves. "I don't think so," he said, flipping through it.

Tommy read from a book on volcanoes. " 'One type of lava has a jagged surface.' "

"Isn't lava black?"

Tommy turned the page. "This one is the right color. 'The release of volcanic gases forms pumice, which is so light it floats in water.' "

On a piece of scrap paper, Gregory wrote "Pumice—floats."

Tommy pulled out *Wonders of the American Desert*.

"He found this thing up north, Tommy."

Tommy wasn't paying attention. " 'In the Petrified Forest, minerals have replaced the wood, perfectly preserving the pattern of the wood grain.' "

Gregory wrote down "Petrified wood—grain."

They kept going. Gregory started to get a stiff neck from reading titles sideways. He got to the next shelf label.

"SEASHORE LIFE. We've gone too far."

Then Gregory saw *Our Universe* on the display shelf. The cover showed a night sky with shooting stars. He raced through the table of contents to "Meteors and Comets."

" 'Meteorites may contain alloys of iron and nickel. Iron meteorites are magnetic.' "

He wrote down "Meteorite—magnetic?"

"The library's closing in five minutes," Mrs. Twombly announced from her desk. "Please bring your books for checkout."

"That's okay," Gregory said, folding the paper. "We've got plenty for now."

Mrs. Nelson closed her book when they walked in. "Your mother phoned. She'll be a little late. Did you get what you needed at the library?"

"I think so. We've got some experiments to do."

Gregory rummaged through his desk and found his magnifying glass and his horseshoe magnet. In the kitchen, he poured water into a mixing bowl and set it on the table.

"Let's try the magnet first," he said, opening the box. For an exciting second, he felt a tug on the magnet, but it was only the cotton ball catching on the metal.

He focused the magnifying glass on the object and examined every part of it.

"Can I try?"

"Sure, but there's no wood grain."

Gregory put the object in the bowl of water. It sank to the bottom.

"Tommy," Mrs. Nelson called from the living room, "what time do you have to be home?"

Tommy looked at the clock. "Uh-oh. Greg, I've got to go." He pulled his jacket on. "Do you want to go back to the library tomorrow?"

"No," Gregory said quietly. "I don't think we'll find anything there."

He walked down the three flights of stairs to the front door with Tommy.

"I was really hoping that thing was a meteorite. See you tomorrow, Greg."

The front door banged shut after him.

After school on Friday, Gregory and Tommy walked around, looking for ideas. At Walker's Garden Shop, they saw bushels of marble chips. At Metro Hardware & Home Center, they saw barrels of gravel.

When they got to Dan the Diver's Tropical Fish, Gregory said, "I'll show you the fish tank I'm going to get."

Dan the Diver had stones—colored ones for aquariums—but nothing like the Mystery Gift.

They walked up to Tommy's corner.

"See you tomorrow, Greg. We're going to put up the Explorer tent, right? You didn't forget, did you?"

Gregory had forgotten. Mostly he'd been thinking about trying to identify Mr. Mayfield's gift. "Sure. I'll be over after breakfast."

"Don't forget the camping book."

Roughing It

*E*arly the next morning, Gregory packed his bag with a length of clothesline and clothespins his mother had given him, a compass, a flashlight, his knot book, and *The Complete Guide to Roughing It.*

He'd found the camping book at a library sale of old books. Some of the pages were torn, but he and Tommy had learned a lot from it, like how to use different kinds of compasses and how to bandage a sprained ankle.

The chapter on tents showed six different kinds—real tents, not the kind he and Tommy had made by pinning blankets together and draping them over the dining-room table. They had decided to start with the Explorer, since that one didn't need a pole, just rope.

"Did you get the clothespins?" Tommy asked when he came to the door.

"Lots. But I have to bring them back."

"That's okay," said Tommy. "My mom says the living room has to be cleaned up by suppertime anyway."

"I've only got one rope."

"Maybe we can use string to hold the tent open. Look. Nonna gave me this old sheet."

They looked for places to tie the rope. Then Gregory noticed the newel post at the top of the staircase leading to the upstairs bedrooms.

"We can use that."

"And we can tie the other end around the dining-room table leg."

By lunchtime, the tent was up. Lengths of string were tied to the sheet and knotted around furniture legs to hold the tent sides apart. It didn't look exactly like the one in the book, since they couldn't stake the strings just where they wanted, but it was a good tent, the best they'd ever made.

"That book sure helps," said Tommy as he crawled into the tent with a plate of tuna-fish sandwiches.

They spent the rest of the afternoon practicing knots and reading about how to build a campfire and put it out with water or dirt.

Gregory paged back to the chapter on tents. "Which one should we put up next time?"

"How about the Voyager?" Tommy said. "That doesn't look too hard."

"I'd like to make the Tepee. You can even cook in a tepee. The smoke goes out the top." Gregory found the page he was looking for. "Here. It says, 'The Tepee is the best tent if you have to live outdoors all year round.' The Indians knew what they were doing."

"That one needs a lot of poles to hold it up. What could we use?"

"We'll figure out something."

"Hey," said Tommy, "did you figure out what Mr. Mayfield sent?"

Gregory shook his head.

"Can you ask somebody?"

"We don't know anybody who knows about rocks."

"Maybe you'll have to give up on this one. You'll get the next one."

Gregory didn't say anything. If he didn't get this one, there wouldn't be a next one.

As he walked home through the early twilight, his mind went round and round. Where could he look for the answer to the mystery? He was out of ideas.

This was the first time Gregory knew somebody who had been to the wilderness. Mr. Mayfield didn't need books. He knew how to fish and use a camp stove. He probably knew all about tents and how to find his way in the woods.

Gregory kicked through some dirty newspaper blowing down the sidewalk. The pink neon sign at Marty's SuperDeli blinked on and off. Horns honked.

Would he ever get to the wilderness himself? As he climbed the hill past Ernie's Used Cars, his dream seemed further off than ever.

That night, before he went to sleep, Gregory slipped the gift out of the box and turned it over in his hand. Mr. Mayfield was right about being careful not to get cut. The thing had sharp edges and ridges where little bits of it seemed to have broken off.

He put the gift back in the box and read the letter once more. "Up north." Towering fir trees and distant howling in the night, the only shelter a snug tepee with a little fire.

Gregory pulled up the covers and turned out the light. He closed his eyes and let himself drift. He was paddling his birchbark canoe silently, surely, down a ●winding river. Birdcalls pierced the dark forest on either side of him. He knew every call.

Suddenly he sat up. He had a wonderful idea, but he couldn't find out if he was right until Monday.

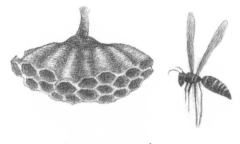

No Reply

At the library on Monday afternoon, Gregory and Tommy skimmed past the books on Native American pottery, dances, ceremonies, tribal dress, customs, and religion.

"Here it is, Tommy! Tools and weapons."

The first chapter had pictures of different kinds of arrowheads.

" 'Arrowheads were often made of flint,' " Tommy read, " 'a glassy mineral which may be gray, brown, or black.' This thing looks glassy, doesn't it, Greg?"

Gregory nodded. Holding his breath, he held the object next to the first picture.

"Well?"

"I'm not sure."

Gregory moved to the second picture, then the third. His first excitement was fading fast. The arrowheads in the book were long and narrow, with perfect points and deep notches.

He turned the page. The bold-type caption caught his eye: "Not all arrowheads have the expected shape." Five oddly shaped specimens were shown. One of them looked exactly like Gregory's. It was a little chunky. The notches didn't match.

"Tommy, we've got it."

That evening, Gregory wrote his next letter.

Dear Mr. Mayfield,

Thank you a million times for the arrowhead. It's the best gift I ever got in my whole life.

Someday Tommy and I are going to make a canoe out of birchbark, just like the Indians did, and take a long trip through the wilderness. First, we're going to learn how to make a tepee and how to track wild animals and set

*up blinds so we can watch them and take pictures of them
and they'll never know we're there.*

*We've planned it for a long time. We're going to
pack sleeping bags and cook all our food over a campfire. I talked it over with Tommy and we'd like you to
come, too, if you can leave the farm for a while.*

Yours,
Greg

He had never told anybody about the plans he
and Tommy had made, not even his mother. Now,
when he wrote to Mr. Mayfield about them, the
words came easily.

This time, he knew what he wanted to send.
That evening, his mother helped him wrap the
paper-wasp nest with more tissue paper. They taped
the box securely, and Gregory printed the address
in big black letters. The next afternoon, he took it
to the post office to be weighed.

He waited anxiously for Mr. Mayfield's next letter to arrive.

When ten days went by, he thought maybe Mr.
Mayfield hadn't been able to get to the post office.

When two weeks went by, he thought maybe Mr. Mayfield didn't have that kind of wasp where he lived. He should have given him a hint. When three weeks went by, he knew why he hadn't gotten a letter—Mr. Mayfield had lost interest.

Gregory tried to keep going with his nature study, but it wasn't fun anymore. He didn't feel like measuring the growth of his grapefruit plant or taking notes on his ant farm. Tommy asked him if he was okay.

He knew his mother was worried. One evening after they'd done the dishes, she sat down with him at the kitchen table.

"Gregory, sometimes grownups just get busy with things. It doesn't mean Mr. Mayfield doesn't care about you."

Gregory looked down at the table and shrugged.

"I hate to see you so miserable. You were having such a good time. I don't think I've ever seen you that happy. I'm sorry I've been working late at the restaurant. I thought I'd better take some overtime. Christmas is coming."

Even thinking about Christmas didn't make Gregory feel any better.

For a minute, his mother didn't say anything.

"It's a shame I had to sell Grandma Kepler's cottage at the lake. You don't remember it, do you, Greg?"

He shook his head. He wished he did remember it. He often took out their album to see the photograph of his father and mother sitting in a rowboat, his father leaning on the oars. He wished he remembered his father, too. Sometimes he had a picture in his mind of a dark-haired man putting yellow mittens on him, but he wasn't sure if he'd dreamed that.

"It's okay," he said. "When I get a job, I'll buy us another one."

His mother smiled. "That's my Greg."

A Telephone Call

As Gregory sat at his desk on Saturday morning, the buzzer sounded. He paid no attention to it. Tommy was at the doctor's for his ear.

"Gregory," his mother called. "A package for you!"

Gregory raced to the front hall.

"See? Mr. Mayfield hasn't forgotten about you."

Under a thick wrapping of brown paper was a sturdy cardboard box. Gregory gently pulled off the lid. Nestled on a bed of shredded paper was a curved object like a giant claw. It was a streaky brown color and hard as stone.

A letter was stuck in the box lid.

Dear Greg,

I'm sorry I've taken so long to write back. I had to turn the house upside-down to find the Mystery Gift I'm sending you. I'd forgotten where I put it after all these years.

I found it on a riverbank near the farm when I was fishing. It was mostly buried in the sand. Might have been washed up by the spring meltwater.

This one's a mystery even to me. At first, I thought it might be a bear tooth, but the vet who takes care of our animals said no, it's too big. Nobody else knew either, so I just put it away, but I never stopped wondering about it.

Reading your letters, I can tell you're serious and determined. I thought maybe somehow you could find out what this is.

Yours,

Pete

P.S. Getting that paper-wasp nest without breaking it must have been quite a trick. Wonderful thing, isn't it?

When Gregory put the open box on Mrs. Twombly's desk later that morning, she stared in amazement. "I'm afraid I don't know what book to give you this time, but I have another idea." She took an address book out of her purse. "My cousin is a professor and he works at the natural history museum. Call him. Maybe he can help." She scribbled on her notepad and handed the top sheet to Gregory.

On it was printed "Dr. George Axelrod" and a phone number.

Gregory put off calling until late afternoon. He dreaded having to talk to this important man. He kept rehearsing what he would say.

After he dialed, the phone rang and rang. He started to hang up when a man's voice came on the line.

"Axelrod here."

"Uh, my name is Gregory Kepler and Mrs. Twombly our librarian said you might be able to help me identify something I got from a friend of mine."

A short silence followed.

"Helen Twombly?" Gregory had never heard her first name before. "Are you sure this isn't something Helen—Mrs. Twombly—can help you with?"

"I'm pretty sure she can't."

"Well, I don't usually see students unless they're in one of my courses at the university . . ."

Gregory felt small and miserable. He'd made a mistake by calling. A professor was too busy to bother with kids.

"That's okay," Gregory said, his voice almost a whisper. "Sorry. 'Bye." He hung up. He felt like a failure.

Mr. Mayfield had trusted him with a special gift, something that he'd kept for years, because he thought that Gregory would search for an answer and wouldn't give up. This might be his only chance to find it.

He put his hand back on the receiver. He worked out a speech and recited it to himself over and over. His hand got sweaty on the phone.

He put the receiver to his ear and dialed. Professor Axelrod came on the line. Gregory took a deep breath.

"It's Gregory Kepler again. I bet you're pretty busy and I wouldn't bother you again, but I really need to find out what this is for a friend of mine. It's a very strange thing and you'd probably think it was interesting if you saw it. It would only take a minute."

This time, Professor Axelrod laughed. "Well, I guess I can spare a whole minute. Stop by next Saturday morning. I'll be here."

After they said goodbye, Gregory stared at the phone. He'd done it. He could hardly believe it.

Back in Time

A cold front blew in the next week. Thanksgiving Day was especially frigid and windy, but Gregory's mind wasn't on the weather. All he could think about was the coming trip to the museum. If Professor Axelrod couldn't help him, what could he do next?

On Saturday morning, Gregory, his mother, and Tommy stood at the number 22 bus stop.

"I hope I'm doing the right thing, letting you and Tommy go alone," Gregory's mother said. "But with two people out sick at the Red Rose, I've got to go in. If only Mrs. Nelson didn't have a cold . . ."

"We'll be okay, Mom. We only have to transfer once."

Gregory wished his mother wouldn't worry so much.

The bus pulled up to the corner. Gregory's mother squeezed his hand. "Okay, sweetheart, just remember—the number 36 at Highland Street."

He and Tommy found seats together. As the bus lumbered down Ridge Street, Gregory could see his mother still waving. He waved and smiled to her so she'd feel better. Then he put his hands back on the package.

Gregory had ridden buses with Tommy lots of times before, but never this far. The only other time they'd been to the museum was on a class trip. A school bus had taken everybody there. It had been a long ride.

At Highland Street, they waited.

"Do you suppose we got off at the right stop?" Tommy asked at last.

"Oh, sure," Gregory said, but he was getting

anxious. Then the number 36 turned the corner. "See? We know what we're doing."

Going through the bronze double doors of the museum was like entering a palace. Their footsteps echoed on the polished marble floor as they walked to the Information desk.

"Yes?" the Information lady's voice echoed.

Gregory handed her the notepaper with the professor's name on it.

"Do you have an appointment?"

Gregory nodded.

"Just a minute. I'll call him. Name, please?"

"Gregory Kepler. And Tommy DeMarco."

After a minute on the phone, the woman pointed. "Go through that door and down the corridor. It's the second door on the left."

They thanked her and started across the big hall to the door marked STAFF ONLY. Looming over them was the massive skeleton of a dinosaur.

"I bet he'd eat you for a snack," said Tommy.

Gregory didn't pay much attention. He was repeating the directions to himself. Down the corridor, second door on the left.

Professor Axelrod was on the phone, but he motioned Gregory and Tommy to come in when he saw them in the doorway. Tommy nudged Gregory. Silently he pointed to a shelf full of animal skulls. A large tortoise shell rested on a stack of books. The professor was toying with a small bone.

"I'll have to get back to you on this metatarsal, Dave. I have two people in my office who need an identification right away." He hung up and smiled. "So, you're the young man I spoke to on the phone. Or one of you is, at least. Now let's see this very interesting object!"

Gregory handed him the box.

"What do we have in here, do you suppose? Couldn't be a *Tyrannosaurus* thighbone," he said with a grin as he weighed it in his hand. "Too light." He lifted the lid. Gregory saw that his manner changed. "Hmmm. This *is* interesting. Wait, I'd better check with—" Suddenly he leaned toward the door. "Jack, got a minute?" he said to a man walking down the corridor. "Could this be what I think it is? A canine tooth from *Smilodon fatalis?*"

The other man examined it closely. "Definitely.

A beautiful specimen. Where did you get this? I'd love to display this in our new Pleistocene exhibit."

Gregory didn't know what "Pleistocene" meant, but it sounded important.

"A friend of mine sent it to me," he said. "He found it when he was fishing. I can show you on a map where he lives."

Gregory turned back to Professor Axelrod. "Could you write down what you said this is so I can tell my friend? I don't think I'll be able to remember it."

For a second, the professor seemed surprised.

"Oh. Didn't I say what *Smilodon fatalis* is? The saber-toothed cat. This is the canine tooth of the most ferocious predator of the Pleistocene Epoch."

When Gregory and Tommy left the museum that day, they had the tooth, an invitation from Professor Axelrod to come for a private tour of the museum, and a letter from Dr. Jack Summersby asking permission from Mr. Mayfield to display his find in the museum's new exhibit, opening in three weeks.

Gregory thought he would explode before his

mother came home and he got to tell her the news. She made cups of cocoa and they had a toast on it before dinner.

That evening, Gregory wrote a letter.

Dear Mr. Mayfield,

You'll never guess what that thing turned out to be. You won't believe me, so please just read the other letter I'm sending in this envelope. I hope you don't faint or anything!

If you say they can put it in the museum, please come stay with us so you can see it. My mother says it's okay, if you can stand sleeping on the fold-out bed in the living room.

I hope you decide to let them show it.

Yours,
Greg

Dear Greg,

Well, I didn't faint, but my wife nearly did. I'm sending back the letter to Dr. Summersby with my signature on it.

You can't imagine what big celebrities we are around

here now. They even sent somebody over from the Ashton *Herald* to interview us.

We'd be happy to come stay with you if you can put up with such big Hollywood stars.

You know, Greg, that I sent the tooth to you as your Mystery Gift, so it's not really mine anymore. I explained to Dr. Summersby about it in the letter.

Yours,

Pete

P.S. We'll only come if you and your mother promise to visit us this summer. Tommy, too! We'll take a canoe trip on the river.

The Silver Balloon

*T*wo weeks later, Gregory stood in front of a glass case full of skulls and bones and plaster models of extinct mammals. On the center shelf was the tooth from the saber-toothed cat. A small white card next to it read: COLLECTION OF MR. CLARENCE MAYFIELD AND MR. GREGORY KEPLER.

Gregory had his back to the glass. In front of him was his whole class and Mr. Hansen. Somewhere behind them stood his mother, Mrs. Nelson, Mr. Mayfield, and Mr. Mayfield's wife, Edith, carrying a camera.

After Tommy had blurted the news to Mr. Hansen and just about everybody else at school, a class trip had been arranged. Gregory had been asked to give a talk. Dr. Summersby had helped him prepare it.

Gregory's mouth was dry. His heart pounded. Then he remembered to look for Mr. Mayfield— Pete. Pete had told him, if he was nervous, to look at him before he started to speak.

Gregory had trouble finding him in the crowd. Then he saw him, standing a little beyond the circle of light from the case. At that moment, Pete gave him a thumbs-up sign, close to his chest. Gregory knew that nobody else saw it. It was a secret signal, just for him.

Gregory swallowed. He cleared his throat. Mr. Hansen shushed everybody. Pete was still holding the thumbs-up sign.

Gregory began.

"The Pleistocene Epoch began about two million years ago and ended about ten thousand years ago. The Pleistocene is also known as the Ice Age. Glaciers advanced and retreated over much of

North America during that time. Mammoths and giant bison roamed the land.

"The most ferocious predator of the Pleistocene Epoch was the saber-toothed cat of the genus *Smilodon,* which means 'knife-toothed.' This animal is often called the saber-toothed tiger, but that is not a good name since it is not a close relative of the tiger, and it may have behaved more like a lion. Scientists think it may have lived and hunted in small groups, the way lions do.

"But the saber-toothed cat was heavier and stronger than a lion. Its neck was especially thick and powerful. The saber teeth could grow up to eight inches long and were probably used to stab and slash prey."

Somebody whispered, "Wow." Growling noises came from the back row.

"Like cats today, the saber-toothed cat was not a good runner, so it probably hunted by stalking. It would sneak up as close as possible to the victim and then"—Gregory paused dramatically, the way he'd rehearsed it with Pete—"pounce!"

He heard a short gasp.

"The saber-toothed cat was especially good at hunting large, slow-moving animals like mastodons and giant ground sloths. It may not have attacked full-grown mastodons, but it did attack younger ones. When its prey animals became extinct at the end of the Ice Age, so did the saber-toothed cat."

He looked up and waited. Mr. Hansen started to applaud.

"Well done, Gregory!"

Suddenly everyone was applauding. Tommy pretended that he'd hurt his hands from clapping so hard. Mrs. Mayfield was pushing Mr. Mayfield up to the front.

"Clarence, stand on the other side. I need a picture for the *Herald*. A little to the left. Now smile . . . smile . . ."

When the photo was developed, it showed a very happy Pete Mayfield and an even happier Gregory Kepler shaking his hand. Framed on the mantelpiece, it was the first thing that Gregory saw when he and his mother and Tommy came to visit the Mayfields that summer.

Next to the photo, Gregory saw something shiny stuffed into a coffee mug. When he looked closer, he saw that it was a piece of plastic—his silver balloon.

Author's Note

I hope Gregory's story inspires readers to pursue their dreams, but in one respect they shouldn't follow his example. Remember that Gregory's balloon floats in the skies of a made-up world. In the real world, helium balloons should not be released outdoors. Harm can come to animals, particularly marine animals, if they swallow or become entangled in the plastic.